Llyfrgelloedd Caerdydd
www.caerdydd.gov.uk/llyfrgelloedd
Cardiff Libraries
www.cardiff.gov.uk/libraries

I'm a bear called Pierre and I love HAIR! From buzz-cuts to bunches to bobs to bouffants and beehives.

I admire the mullet.

I mull over mohawks.

I have a penchant for
pigtails and ponytails . . .

I'd even try a whale-tail.
I love them all!

When my hair looks fantastic,
I FEEL fantastic! Just like my
favourite roller disco team . . .

# THE POODLE SQUAD!
## They have the most fantastic hair!

I want to show the world that a bear can have fantastic hair too. With a perfect quiff . . .

I'd be able to perform an ultra dazzling roller-skating lift with my own skating squad.

When the news spread that The Poodle Squad would be judging this year's Roller Stars Championships we could barely contain ourselves!

We began training right away!

To impress the Poodle Squad it takes strength . . .

knowledge . . .

agility . . .

and determination.

We trained for weeks. There were many hair-styles, fur balls and tears.

But nothing could stop us.

All we needed now was the perfect look.

But when the big day came,
whatever I tried, my hair was
never enough!

Don bounced impatiently, ready to leave, but my quiff still needed more lift!

Jon yelped that it was time to go but my fringe still needed more zhuzh!

Yvonne gave me a spikey prod and squeaked "We're late to our big show!"
But I just needed one more minute to perfect my style . . .

Finally I was ready to go!
But my friends had GONE!

And now I was LATE! I could still make it
if I got a wriggle on . . .

The road to the roller disco was so long and winding.
It would take me forever to get there!

Then I had a great idea! I'd get there much quicker
if I took a shortcut down the hill!

I plunged into the mud!

I sprang through the bushes!

I soared across the sky!

Vaulted over beehives . . .

and slid
under udders!

I was
almost there . . .

After a record-breaking race against time I finally arrived and I leapt straight into the rink to join my squad!

The crowd gasped . . .

"Oh no! My HAIR!"
The crowd was silent.
The Poodle Squad stared.
My knees wobbled.

"Are you OK?" asked Don.
Jon and Yvonne gave me a
warm wave, cheering me on.

Their friendly faces reminded
me exactly why I was there . . .
I was there to skate with
my friends!

"Yes!" I cheered "Let's skate
our hearts out."

The crowd went wild! And The Poodle Squad did too!

It was the most fun I'd had in ages!

It turns out I don't need good hair
to have a great time . . .

All I need is my friends!

But I have heard rumours of a wild new craze
sweeping through town . . .

Dedicated to everyone
chasing their dreams...

With special thanks to my
family and friends who
encourage me to pursue mine.

**Thank you to Helen, Pam,
Martin, Hannah, Alice, Mick,
Emilia and Fay for guidance
along the way.**

First published 2021 by order of the Tate Trustees
by Tate Publishing, a division of Tate Enterprises Ltd,
Millbank, London SW1P 4RG

www.tate.org.uk/publishing

A catalogue record for this book is available from the British Library

HB ISBN 978 1 84976 746 0

PB ISBN 978 1 84976 771 2

Distributed in the United States and Canada by ABRAMS, New York
Library of Congress Control Number applied for

Colour reproduction by Evergreen Colour Management Ltd
Printed and bound in China by C&C Offset Printing Co., Ltd